A Beginning-to-Read Book

Very Important People

by Mary Lindeen

NORWOOD HOUSE PRESS

DEAR CAREGIVER, The *Beginning to Read—Read and Discover* books provide emergent readers the opportunity to explore the world through nonfiction while building early reading skills. The text integrates both common sight words and content vocabulary. These key words are featured on lists provided at the back of the book to help your child expand his or her sight word recognition, which helps build reading fluency. The content words expand vocabulary and support comprehension.

Nonfiction text is any text that is factual. The Common Core State Standards call for an increase in the amount of informational text reading among students. The Standards aim to promote college and career readiness among students. Preparation for college and career endeavors requires proficiency in reading complex informational texts in a variety of content areas. You can help your child build a foundation by introducing nonfiction early. To further support the CCSS, you will find Reading Reinforcement activities at the back of the book that are aligned to these Standards.

Above all, the most important part of the reading experience is to have fun and enjoy it!

Sincerely,

Shannon Cannon

Shannon Cannon, Ph.D.
Literacy Consultant

Norwood House Press
Chicago, Illinois
For more information about Norwood House Press please visit our website at
www.norwoodhousepress.com or call 866-565-2900.
© 2020 Norwood House Press. Beginning-to-Read™ is a trademark of Norwood House Press.
All rights reserved. No part of this book may be reproduced or utilized in any form or by any
means without written permission from the publisher.

Editor: Judy Kentor Schmauss
Designer: Sara Radka

Photo Credits:
Getty Images, 1–7, 9–13, 15–24, 26–29; Shutterstock, 8, 14, 25, 27

Library of Congress Cataloging-in-Publication Data
Names: Lindeen, Mary, author.
Title: Very important people / by Mary Lindeen.
Description: Chicago, Illinois : Norwood House Press, [2020] |
    Series: A beginning-to-read book | Audience: 5-8. | Audience: K to 3.
Identifiers: LCCN 2018054640 | ISBN 9781684509409 (hardcover) |
    ISBN 9781684044238 (pbk.) | ISBN 9781684044283 (ebook)
Subjects: LCSH: Community life–Juvenile literature. | Human services personnel–Juvenile literature. |
    Communities–Juvenile literature.
Classification: LCC HM761 .L559 2020 | DDC 307–dc23
LC record available at https://lccn.loc.gov/2018054640

Hardcover ISBN: 978-1-68450-940-9
Paperback ISBN: 978-1-68404-423-8

319N—072019
Manufactured in the United States of America in North Mankato, Minnesota.

Welcome to our community!

Let's meet some of the very
important people who live here.

This is our mayor.

She's the leader
of our town.

She helps make
the rules for
our community.

Our police officers make sure
everyone follows the law.

They also help keep us safe.

Our firefighters help keep us safe, too.

They put out fires and they rescue people.

Our doctors help all of us stay healthy.

Our dentists do, too.

Architects design buildings that
are safe for us to live and work in.

Then carpenters build them.

Artists in our community create art, music, and dances for all of us to enjoy together.

Our mail carriers deliver the mail to everyone.

They keep our community connected.

Our garbage collectors pick up the trash.

They keep our community clean.

Our bus drivers
take us where
we need to go.

Our farmers feed us.

They grow the food that we eat.

And when we eat out, chefs cook the food for us!

Taking care of the kids in our community is very important work.

Families take care of their kids at home.

Teachers take care of kids at school.

Who else
is important in
our community?

Kids are!

Kids help at home
and at school.

They help inside
and outside.

Everyone in a community is important!

. . . READING REINFORCEMENT. . .

CRAFT AND STRUCTURE

To check your child's understanding of this book, recreate the following two-column chart on a sheet of paper. Read the book with your child, and then help him or her fill in the chart using what they learned. Work together to complete the chart by adding rows for the remaining important community people and jobs:

Important Person	Important Person's Job
Mayor	
Firefighter	
Police Officer	
Doctor	

VOCABULARY: Learning Content Words

Content words are words that are specific to a particular topic. All of the content words in this book can be found on page 32. Use some or all of these content words to complete one or more of the following activities:

- Ask your child about the words using questions that begin with "Who?" "What?" "Where?" "When?" "Why?" and "How?"

- Play "Jeopardy" with your child. Give answers that are clues to content words, and then have your child come up with the matching questions; for example, A: This person grows our food. Q: Who is a *farmer*?

- Ask your child to draw pictures of words he or she has difficulty remembering the meaning to.

- Have your child find smaller words or word parts within the words.

- Say a word and have your child say the first word that comes to mind. Discuss the connection between his or her answer and the content word.

FOUNDATIONAL SKILLS: Multisyllabic words

Multisyllabic words are words with more than one syllable. Have your child identify the number of syllables in each of the words below. Then ask your child to find multisyllabic words in this book.

important	firefighters	dentists
community	everyone	carpenters
officers	rescue	carriers

CLOSE READING OF INFORMATIONAL TEXT

Close reading helps children comprehend text. It includes reading a text, discussing it with others, and answering questions about it. Use these questions to discuss this book with your child:

- Who would you call if someone took your bike?
- How do dentists help people?
- Why are bus drivers an important job in a community?
- Who takes care of kids at school? How do they do it?
- How are farmers and chefs similar?
- Which job would you like to have? Why?

FLUENCY

Fluency is the ability to read accurately with speed and expression. Help your child practice fluency by using one or more of the following activities:

- Reread the book to your child at least two times while he or she uses a finger to track each word as it is read.
- Read a line of the book, then reread it as your child reads along with you.
- Ask your child to go back through the book and read the words he or she knows.
- Have your child practice reading the book several times to improve accuracy, rate, and expression.

··· Word List ···

Very Important People uses the 103 words listed below. *High-frequency words* are those words that are used most often in the English language. They are sometimes referred to as sight words because children need to learn to recognize them automatically when they read. *Content words* are any words specific to a particular topic. Regular practice reading these words will enhance your child's ability to read with greater fluency and comprehension.

High-Frequency Words

a	go	out	their	us
all	help(s)	people	them	very
also	here	put	then	we
and	home	school	they	when
are	in	she	this	where
at	is	some	to	who
do	make	take(ing)	together	work
eat	of	that	too	
for	our	the	up	

Content Words

architects	cook	farmers	kids	pick
art(ists)	create	feed	law	police
build(ings)	dances	firefighters	leader	rescue
bus	deliver	fires	let's	rules
care	dentists	follows	live	safe
carpenters	design	food	mail	she's
carriers	doctors	garbage	mayor	stay
chefs	drivers	grow	meet	sure
clean	else	healthy	music	teachers
collectors	enjoy	important	need	town
community	everyone	inside	officers	trash
connected	families	keep	outside	welcome

••• About the Author

Mary Lindeen is a writer, editor, parent, and former elementary school teacher. She has written more than 100 books for children and edited many more. She specializes in early literacy instruction and books for young readers, especially nonfiction.